Turtle and Snake Fix It

A Viking Easy-to-Read

by Kate Spohn

VIKING

For Steve, who is good with tools

VIKING
Published by the Penguin Group
Penguin Putnam Books for Young Readers,
345 Hudson Street, New York, New York 10014, U.S.A.
Penguin Books Ltd, 27 Wrights Lane, London W8 5TZ, England
Penguin Books Australia Ltd, Ringwood, Victoria, Australia
Penguin Books Canada Ltd, 10 Alcorn Avenue, Toronto, Ontario, Canada M4V 3B2
Penguin Books (N.Z.) Ltd, 182-190 Wairau Road, Auckland 10, New Zealand

Penguin Books Ltd, Registered Offices: Harmondsworth, Middlesex, England

First published in 2002 by Viking,
a division of Penguin Putnam Books for Young Readers.

1 3 5 7 9 10 8 6 4 2

LIBRARY OF CONGRESS CATALOGING-IN-PUBLICATION DATA
Spohn, Kate.
Turtle and Snake fix it / by Kate Spohn.
p. cm.
Summary: Turtle tries out his new tools at Snake's house, but when he is
finished fixing things there may be even more work to do.
ISBN 0-670-03540-8 (hardcover)
[1. Repairing—Fiction. 2. Turtles—Fiction. 3. Snakes—Fiction.] I. Title.
PZ7.S7636 Tut 2002   [E]—dc21   2001002866

Viking®, and Easy-to-Read®, are registered trademarks of Penguin Putnam Inc.

Printed in Hong Kong
Set in Bookman

Reading Level 2.0

Turtle and Snake
Fix It

One morning, Turtle opens
his windows.
He smells flowers blooming.

He hears birds singing.

He sees buds on the trees.

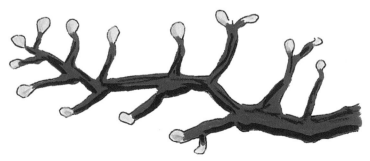

Spring is here.
Time for Turtle to try out
his new tools!

So Turtle puts on his hard hat,

his tool belt,

and his work boots.

Then he goes to Snake's house.
Knock! Knock!
"I've come to fix things," says Turtle.

8

SNAKE

"What things?" asks Snake.
"Anything broken," says Turtle.

9

"This shelf tilts to the left,"
says Snake.
"I can fix the shelf," says Turtle.

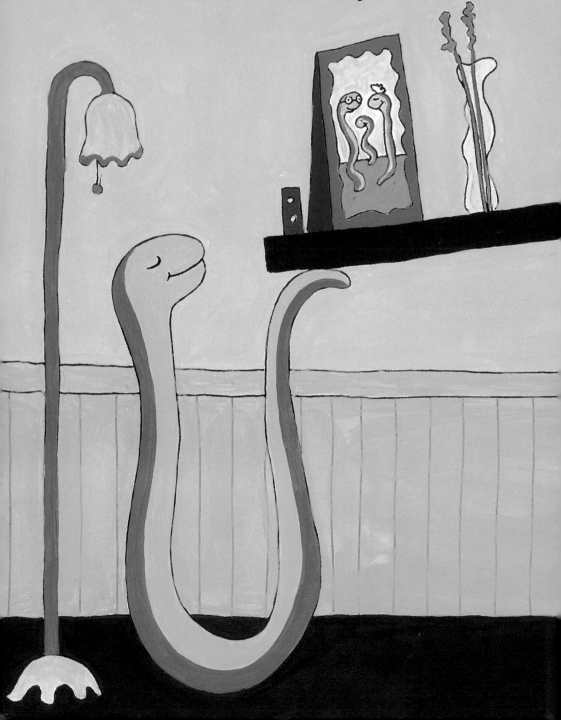

Tap, tap, tap goes the hammer.

"There," says Turtle.
"Now the shelf tilts to the right!"

"What else?" asks Turtle.
"This chair leg is short," says Snake.

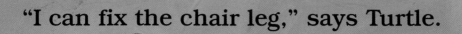
"I can fix the chair leg," says Turtle.

14

Cut, cut, cut goes the saw.

"There," says Turtle. "Now
all the chair legs are the same!"

"This closet door is hard to open," says Snake.

"I can fix the closet door,"
says Turtle.

Turn, turn, turn goes the screwdriver.

"There," says Turtle. "Now the
closet door is easy to open!"

"Let's take a cookie break,"
says Snake.
"Wait," says Turtle. "Do I
hear a *drip, drip*?"

21

"Yes," says Snake. "The pipe
is dripping."
"I can fix the pipe," says Turtle.

Twist, twist, twist goes the wrench.

"There," says Turtle.
"Now the pipe isn't dripping."

24

"This wallpaper is peeling,"
says Snake.

"I can fix the wallpaper," says Turtle.

Swipe, swipe, swipe goes the brush.

"There," says Turtle. "Now
the wallpaper isn't peeling."

"Turtle, thank you for all your help," says Snake.
"I like fixing things," says Turtle.

"I'd like to build a tree house next," says Turtle.

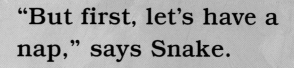

"But first, let's have a nap," says Snake.

And that's just what they do.